P9-AFZ-727

The CHRISTMAS MIRACLE *of* JONATHAN TOOMEY

The CHRISTMAS MIRACLE *of* JONATHAN TOOMEY

SUSAN WOJCIECHOWSKI

ILLUSTRATED BY

P.J. LYNCH

CANDLEWICK PRESS

For Joel, with love
S. W.

For Fran and Ada

With special thanks to
Nicole and Nicholas and Jack
and the Shelburne Museum, Vermont

P.J. L.

T HE VILLAGE CHILDREN
CALLED HIM MR. GLOOMY.

But, in fact, his name was Toomey, Mr. Jonathan Toomey. And though it's not kind to call people names, this one fit quite well. For Jonathan Toomey seldom smiled and never laughed. He went about mumbling and grumbling, muttering and sputtering, grumping and griping. He complained that the church bells rang too often, that the birds sang too shrilly, that the children played too loudly.

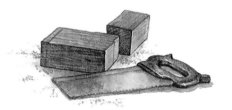

Mr. Toomey was a woodcarver. Some said he was the best woodcarver in the whole valley. He spent his days sitting at a workbench, carving beautiful shapes from blocks of pine and hickory and chestnut wood. After supper, he sat in a straight-backed chair near the fireplace, smoking his pipe and staring into the flames.

Jonathan Toomey wasn't an old man, but if you saw him, you might think he was, the way he walked bent forward with his head down. You wouldn't notice his eyes, the clear blue of an August sky. And you wouldn't see the dimple on his chin, since his face was mostly hidden under a shaggy, untrimmed beard, speckled with sawdust and wood shavings and, depending what he ate that day, with crumbs of bread or a bit of potato or dried gravy.

The village people didn't know it, but there was a reason for his gloom, a reason for his grumbling, a reason why he walked hunched over, as if carrying a great weight on his shoulders. Some years earlier, when Jonathan Toomey was young and full of life and full of love, his wife and baby had become very sick. And, because those were the days before hospitals and medicines and skilled doctors, his wife and baby died, three days apart from each other.

So Jonathan Toomey had packed his belongings into a wagon and traveled till his tears stopped. He settled into a tiny house at the edge of a village to do his woodcarving.

One day in early December, there was a knock at Jonathan's door. Mumbling and grumbling, he went to answer it. There stood a woman and a young boy.

"I'm the widow McDowell. I'm new in your village. This is my son, Thomas," the woman said.

"I'm seven and I know how to whistle," said Thomas.

"Whistling is pish-posh," said the woodcarver gruffly.

"I need something carved," said the woman, and she told Jonathan about a very special set of Christmas figures her grandfather had carved for her when she was a girl.

"After I moved here, I discovered that they were lost," she explained. "I had hoped that by some miracle I would find them again, but it hasn't happened."

"There are no such things as miracles," the woodcarver told her. "Now, could you describe the figures for me?"

"There were sheep," she told him.

"Two of them, with curly wool," added Thomas.

"Yes, two," said the widow, "and a cow, an angel, Mary, Joseph, the Baby Jesus, and the wise men."

"Three of them," added Thomas.

"Will you take the job?" asked the widow McDowell.

"I will."

"I'm grateful. How soon can you have them ready?"

"They will be ready when they are ready," he said.

"But I must have them by Christmas. They mean very much to me. I can't remember a Christmas without them."

"Christmas is pish-posh," said Jonathan gruffly, and he shut the door.

The following week there was a knock at the woodcarver's door. Muttering and sputtering, he went to answer it. There stood the widow McDowell and Thomas.

"Excuse me," said the widow, "but Thomas has been begging to come and watch you work. He says he wants to be a woodcarver when he grows up and would like to watch you since you are the best in the valley."

"I'll be quiet. You won't even know I'm here. Please, please," piped in Thomas.

With a grumble, the woodcarver stepped aside to let them in. He pointed to a stool near his workbench. "No talking, no jiggling, no noise," he ordered Thomas.

The widow McDowell handed Mr. Toomey a warm loaf of corn bread as a token of thanks. Then she took out her knitting and sat down in a rocking chair in the far corner of the cottage.

"Not there!" bellowed the woodcarver. "No one sits in that chair." So she moved to the straight-backed chair by the fire.

Thomas sat very still. Once, when he needed to sneeze, he pressed a finger under his nose to hold it back. Once, when he wanted desperately to scratch his leg, he counted to twenty to keep his mind off the itch.

After a very long time, Thomas cleared his throat and whispered, "Mr. Toomey, may I ask a question?"

The woodcarver glared at Thomas, then shrugged his shoulders and grunted. Thomas decided it meant "yes," so he went on. "Is that my sheep you're carving?"

The woodcarver nodded and grunted again.

After another very long time, Thomas whispered, "Mr. Toomey, excuse me, but you're carving my sheep wrong."

The widow McDowell's knitting needles stopped clicking. Jonathan Toomey's knife stopped carving. Thomas went on. "It's a beautiful sheep, nice and curly, but my sheep looked happy."

"That's pish-posh," said Mr. Toomey. "Sheep are sheep. They cannot look happy."

"Mine did," said Thomas. "They knew they were with the Baby Jesus, so they were happy."

After that, Thomas was quiet for the rest of the afternoon. When the church bells chimed six o'clock, Mr. Toomey grumbled under his breath about the awful noise. The widow McDowell said it was time to leave. Thomas sneezed three times, then thanked the woodcarver for allowing him to watch.

That evening, after a supper of corn bread and boiled potatoes, the woodcarver sat down at his bench. He picked up his knife. He picked up the sheep. He worked until his eyelids drooped shut.

A few days later there was a knock at the woodcarver's door. Griping and grumbling, he went to answer it. There stood the widow and her son.

"May I watch again? I will be quiet," said Thomas.

He settled himself on the stool very quietly, while his mother laid a basket of sweet-smelling raisin buns on the table.

"The teapot is warm," Mr. Toomey said gruffly, his head bent over his work.

While Mr. Toomey carved, the widow McDowell poured tea. She touched the woodcarver gently on the shoulder and placed a cup of tea and a bun next to him. He pretended not to notice, but soon, both the plate and the cup were empty.

Thomas tried to eat the bun his mother had given him as quietly as he could. But it is almost impossible to be seven and eat a warm sticky raisin bun without making various smacking, licking, satisfied noises.

When Thomas had finished, he tried to sit quietly. Once, he almost hiccupped, but he took a deep breath and held it till his face turned red. And once, without thinking, he began to swing his legs, but a glare from the woodcarver stopped him and he kept them so still they fell asleep.

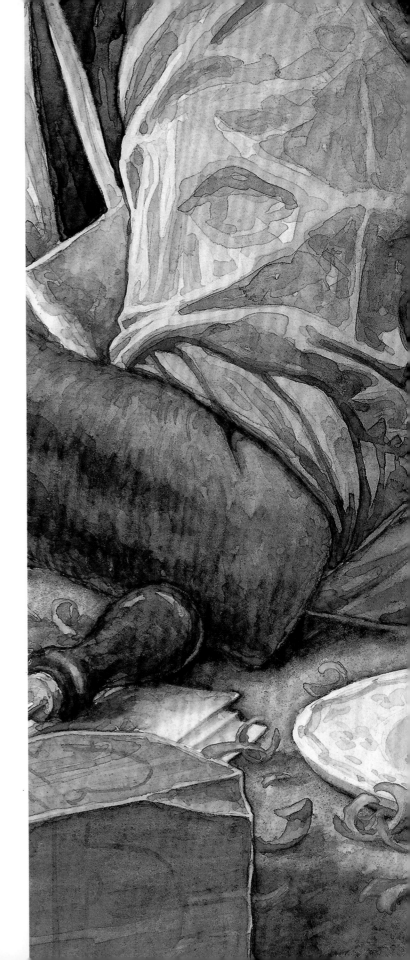

After a very long time, Thomas whispered, "Mr. Toomey, excuse me, may I ask a question?"

Grunt.

"Is that my cow you're carving?"

Nod and grunt.

Another very long time went by. Then Thomas cleared his throat and said, "Mr. Toomey, excuse me, but I must tell you something. That is a beautiful cow, the most beautiful cow I have ever seen, but it's not right. My cow looked proud."

"That's pish-posh," growled the woodcarver. "Cows are cows. They cannot look proud."

"My cow did. It knew that Jesus chose to be born in its barn, so it was proud."

Thomas was quiet for the rest of the afternoon. The only sounds that could be heard were the scraping of the carving knife, the humming of the widow McDowell, and the *click-click* of her knitting needles.

When the church bells chimed six o'clock, Mr. Toomey muttered under his breath about the noise. The widow McDowell said it was time to leave. Thomas shook first one leg, then the other. He thanked the woodcarver for allowing him to watch.

That evening, after a supper of boiled potatoes and raisin buns, the woodcarver sat down at his bench. He picked up his carving knife. He picked up the cow. He worked until his eyelids drooped shut.

A few days later there was a knock on the woodcarver's door. He smoothed down his hair as he went to answer it. At the door were the widow and her son.

"May I watch again?" asked Thomas.

As Mrs. McDowell warmed the tea and put a plate of fresh molasses cookies on the workbench, Thomas watched the woodcarver work on the figure of an angel.

After a very long time, Thomas spoke. "Mr. Toomey, excuse me, is that my angel you're carving?"

"Yes. And would you do me the favor of telling me exactly what I'm doing wrong?"

"Well, my angel looked like one of God's most important angels, because it was sent to Baby Jesus."

"And just how does one make an angel look important?" asked the woodcarver.

"You'll be able to do it," said Thomas. "You are the best woodcarver in the valley."

After another very long time, Thomas spoke. "Mr. Toomey, excuse me, may I ask a question?"

"Do you ever stop talking?" asked the woodcarver.

"My mother says I don't. She says I could learn about the virtue of silence from you."

Under his beard, the woodcarver's face turned pink.

The widow McDowell's face turned as red as the scarf she was knitting.

"Well, speak up, what is your question?"

"Will you please teach me to carve?"

"I am a very busy man," grumbled the woodcarver. But he put down the important angel. "You will carve a bird."

"A robin, I hope," said Thomas. "I like robins."

With a piece of charcoal, the woodcarver sketched a robin on a piece of brown paper. He handed Thomas a small block of pine and a knife. He showed him how to lop the corners from the block and slowly smooth the edges of the wood into curves.

Thomas copied the woodcarver's strokes, head bent, tongue working from side to side of his lower lip as he concentrated.

When the church bells chimed six o'clock, Jonathan Toomey was holding Thomas's hand in his, guiding the knife along the edge of a wing. He didn't hear them ringing. The widow McDowell said it was time to leave. Thomas brushed wood shavings from his shirt. Then he reached out and brushed two especially large pieces of wood shaving from Jonathan Toomey's beard. He thanked the woodcarver for teaching him how to carve.

Later, after a supper of boiled potatoes and molasses cookies, Jonathan Toomey went to his workbench. He thought for a long time. He sketched drawing after drawing. Finally, he picked up his carving knife. He picked up the angel. He carved until his eyelids drooped shut.

A few days later there was a knock on the woodcarver's door. Mr. Toomey jumped up to answer it.

There stood the widow McDowell with a bouquet of pine boughs and holly sprigs, dotted with berries. And there stood Thomas, clutching his partly carved robin.

While Thomas and Mr. Toomey carved, Mrs. McDowell put the branches in a jar of water. She scrubbed Mr. Toomey's kitchen table and set the jar in the center, on a pretty cloth embroidered with lilies of the valley and daisies, which she found in a drawer below the cupboard.

"Next, I will carve the wise men and Joseph," the woodcarver said to Thomas. "Perhaps, before I begin, you will tell me about all the mistakes I am going to make."

"Well," said Thomas, "my wise men were wearing their most wonderful robes because they were going to visit Jesus, and my Joseph was leaning over Baby Jesus like he was protecting him. He looked very serious."

It wasn't until the church bells had chimed that Mr. Toomey saw the jar of pine branches and the cloth embroidered with lilies of the valley and daisies.

"I found the cloth in a drawer. I thought it would look pretty on the table," the widow McDowell said, smiling.

"Never open that drawer," the woodcarver said harshly.

When the two had left, Jonathan folded the cloth and put it back in the drawer below the cupboard.

That evening, after a supper of boiled potatoes, the woodcarver worked on Joseph and the wise men until his eyelids drooped shut.

A few days later there was a knock on the woodcarver's door. He dusted the crumbs from his beard and brushed the sawdust from his shirt. At the door were the widow McDowell and Thomas.

All afternoon Thomas watched the woodcarver work. When it was time to leave, Jonathan said to Thomas, "I am about to begin the last two figures—Mary and the baby. Can you tell me how your figures looked?"

"They were the most special of all," said Thomas. "Jesus was smiling and reaching up to his mother, and Mary looked like she loved him very much."

"Thank you, Thomas," said the woodcarver.

"Tomorrow is Christmas. Is there any chance the figures will be ready?" the widow McDowell asked.

"They will be ready when they are ready."

"I understand," said the widow, and she handed Jonathan two packages. "Merry Christmas," she said.

Jonathan folded his arms across his chest. "I want no presents," he said harshly.

"That is exactly why we are giving them," answered the widow. She put them on the table and left.

Jonathan sat down at the table. Slowly, he opened the first package. Inside was a red scarf, hand-knit, warm and bright. He tied the scarf around his neck.

The other parcel held a robin, crudely carved of pine. A smile twitched at the corners of Jonathan's mouth as he ran his fingers over the lopsided wings. He dusted the fireplace mantel with his sleeve and placed the robin exactly in the center, so he could look at it from his chair.

The woodcarver did not eat supper that day. Instead he began to sketch the final figures, Mary and Jesus. He drew Mary, then wadded the sketch into a ball and tossed it on the floor. He drew the baby, wadded the sketch into a ball, and tossed it with the first. He sketched again. Once more he crumpled the paper. Soon there was a small mountain of crumpled papers at his feet. He picked up a block of wood and tried to carve, but his knife would not do what he wanted it to do. He hurled the chunk of wood into the fireplace and sat, staring into the flames.

When he heard the church bells announcing the midnight Christmas service, he got up. Slowly he opened the drawer beneath the cupboard, the drawer he had told the widow never to open.

From it he took the cloth embroidered with lilies of the valley and daisies. He took out a rough woolen shawl and a lace handkerchief. He took out a tiny white baby blanket and a little pair of blue socks. He placed each piece gently on the floor. From the bottom of the drawer he lifted out a picture frame, beautifully carved of deep-brown chestnut wood.

In the frame was a charcoal sketch of a woman sitting in a rocking chair, holding a baby. The baby's arms were reaching up, touching the woman's face. The woman was looking down at the baby, smiling. Jonathan sat down in his rocking chair and held the picture against his chest. He rocked slowly, his eyes closed. Two tears trailed into his beard.

When he finally took the picture to his workbench and began to carve, his fingers worked quickly and surely. He carved all through the night.

The next day, there was a knock on the widow McDowell's door.

When she opened it, there stood the woodcarver, his neck wrapped in a red scarf, holding a wooden box stuffed with straw.

"Mr. Toomey!" said the widow. "What a surprise. Merry Christmas."

"The figures are ready," he said as he stepped inside. From the box, Jonathan unpacked two curly sheep, happy sheep because they were with Jesus. He unpacked a proud cow and an angel, a very important angel with mighty wings stretching from its shoulders right down to the hem of its gown. He unpacked three wise men wearing their most wonderful robes, edged with fur and falling in rich folds.

He unpacked a serious and caring Joseph. He unpacked Mary wearing a rough woolen shawl, looking down, loving her precious baby son. Jesus was smiling and reaching up to touch his mother's face.

That day, Jonathan went to the Christmas service with the widow McDowell and Thomas. And that day in the churchyard the village children saw Jonathan throw back his head, showing his eyes as clear blue as an August sky, and laugh. No one ever called him Mr. Gloomy again.

SUSAN WOJCIECHOWSKI

The Christmas Miracle of Jonathan Toomey has been a miracle in my life.

I have always believed in the existence of a higher power than we mortals, and this higher power must have played a hand in its creation. I wrote the story when I was a school librarian and wanted to read my students a story that expressed what was, for me, the message of Christmas: hope. Beyond that I have no memory of the actual writing of the story. Instead of the mountain of drafts, revisions, and edits that accompanied the creation of each of my other books, for this one I have just a few sheets of paper as witness to the fact that I indeed wrote the story. Then, when the story was accepted for publication by Candlewick Press, almost no changes were suggested by my gifted and supremely capable editor, Amy Ehrlich. This is almost unheard of in the publishing business. Instead, I received a letter stating, "Your story is just about perfect." Also highly unusual, I was asked to choose an illustrator. After much research, I chose the talented P.J. Lynch, and miraculously, he accepted. He is truly a master of his art. When I first saw the finished illustrations, they touched me so deeply that tears ran down my face as I turned the pages.

Authors generally like what they write, but never know if the rest of the world will. So when the book was released, I decided to just sit back and enjoy whatever ride lay ahead. It has been quite a ride. Because of *Toomey,* I have traveled the country, witnessed the creation of dramatic and film adaptations of the story, seen the book translated into numerous languages, and attended the Grammy awards when James Earl Jones's audio reading of the book was nominated. But most memorable have been the people I've met on the twenty-year journey. I met a woman who told me she had bought my book at a conference, then read it aloud that night with her husband. The next day he went out for a motorcycle ride and was killed. The woman believed she had been destined to read that story at that precise time because its message gave her the strength to move forward. She knew that in time, despite her anguish, everything would be all right. I met a teacher who talked to me about how perceptive children are. She had read the book to her first-graders, then asked questions. When she asked what Jonathan Toomey had taken from a drawer, a child answered, "He took his heart out of the drawer." When you read the book, you'll understand the profound depth of that child's answer.

A high point in the journey was the day the CD of James Earl Jones reading my story arrived in the mail. I immediately rounded up my husband and three children to listen to it as a family. When Jones's powerful reading ended, I saw a look of pride and awe in my children's eyes. If you're a parent, you know these moments don't come easily or often. I was smiling, ready for my moment in the sun. I knew they finally realized that their mom was pretty special. With breathless awe they gushed, "Mom, Darth Vader said your name!"

Yes, it's been quite a ride. My thanks to Candlewick for their unending support, and to all of you who have shared in my miracle over the past twenty years.

P.J. LYNCH

I was excited when I was asked to provide a new painting for the cover of this, the 20th anniversary edition of *The Christmas Miracle of Jonathan Toomey*. But it was strange for me to revisit those characters I had spent so much time with two decades before.

I dug out the old photos I had taken of my friends acting out the roles of Toomey, the widow McDowell and her son, Thomas. I found lots of photos I had taken of early American buildings, and of old tools of the type that a woodcarver might have used, and I remembered back to the first time I read Susan's story.

It had been immediately clear to me that *The Christmas Miracle of Jonathan Toomey* was a very special story. I had never read such a moving and beautifully paced text. But it wasn't at all like any of the fairy-tale books I had illustrated before: no princesses, monsters, or castles. For a time I doubted whether I was the right artist to illustrate it. But Susan had chosen me, and the more I reread it, the more I could visualize how the book might look, and the more I wanted to be the one who would create the pictures for it.

All the research I did was useful for working my way into the project. But I knew that my real challenge was not to do with costumes or tools; it was to try to match, in my pictures, the deep emotional core of Susan's story, to try to somehow show what might be going on inside a character's head, or inside his heart.

There was a good year of work in my paintings for this book, and there were nights when, like Jonathan Toomey, I worked on into the early hours, until my eyelids drooped shut.

I can't say whether my work on *The Christmas Miracle of Jonathan Toomey* was inspired in the same mystical way that Susan's was. But it is true to say that as I painted, I had no doubts, and that is very unusual for me.

The book's huge success has changed my life and career for the better in many ways. It has meant that I have traveled widely, particularly in the U.S., and I have met many people who love this book and who have made it a part of their family's Christmas each year. Hearing them tell what this book means to them has been a joyful and humbling experience.

In the twenty years since the book was first published, Susan and I have grown older, but the book is as fresh and its message of hope is as powerful today as it was back then. It is a rare and special privilege to have shared in the creation of such a wonderful thing as *The Christmas Miracle of Jonathan Toomey*.

Text copyright © 1995 by Susan Wojciechowski

Illustrations copyright © 1995 by P.J. Lynch

First edition in this format 2015

Library of Congress Catalog Card Number 94-048917

ISBN 978-0-7636-7822-7

18 19 20 CCP 10 9 8 7 6 5 4

Printed in Shenzhen, Guangdong, China

This book was typeset in Columbus MT.

The illustrations were done in watercolor.

Candlewick Press

99 Dover Street

Somerville, Massachusetts 02144

visit us at www.candlewick.com